# Daddy Kiss

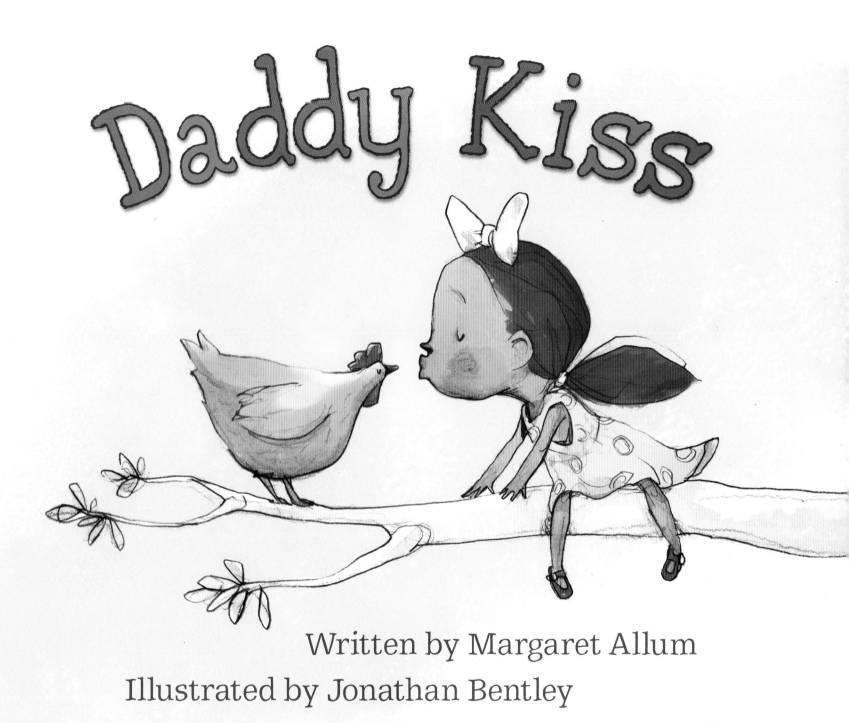

Written by Margaret Allum

Illustrated by Jonathan Bentley

LITTLE HARE
www.littleharebooks.com

For Imogen – MA

For Ruby and Harvey – JB

Little Hare Books
an imprint of
Hardie Grant Egmont
85 High Street
Prahran, Victoria 3181, Australia

www.littleharebooks.com

Text copyright © Little Hare Books 2010
Illustrations copyright © Jonathan Bentley 2010
Text written by Margaret Allum

First published 2010

National Library of Australia
Cataloguing-in-Publication entry

Allum, Margaret.
Daddy kiss / Margaret Allum; illustrator, Jonathan Bentley.
9781921541308 (hbk.)
For pre-school age.
Kissing – Juvenile fiction.
Fathers – Juvenile fiction.
Bentley, Jonathan.
A823.4

Designed by Vida & Luke Kelly
Produced by Pica Digital, Singapore
Printed through Phoenix Offset
Printed in Shen Zhen, Guangdong Province, China, May 2010
5 4 3 2 1

I like kisses.

I like big kisses ...

and small kisses ...

and pecky kisses ...

and smoochy, lip-smacky kisses.

I kiss the cat for a fluffy kiss ...

and the dog for a waggly kiss.

I kiss flowers for a petal kiss...

butterflies for a fluttery kiss ...

dandelions for a whiskery kiss …

and snowflakes
for a frosty kiss.

I kiss after squabbling for a sorry kiss ...

and after playing
for a friendly kiss …

before leaving for a sad kiss ...

and when arriving
for a hello kiss.

I sometimes like a
smelly-yelly-brother-kiss …

and I often get a rosy-cosy-granny-kiss …

and I always want a
snuggly-cuddly-mummy-kiss.

But the kiss I love most is a
great, big bristly-growly-daddy-kiss!

That's my favourite kiss of all.